D1449330

OPEN YOUR HEART

Written by Layne A.L. Pecoff

Paintings by Grant Pecoff

RISING
LYONS
PRESS

www.risinglyonspress.com

Open Your Heart, Second Edition
Copyright © 2005, 2007
by Layne A.L. Pecoff and Grant Pecoff

Library of Congress Number: 2007922407

First Printing, April 2005
ISBN: 978-0-9793492-0-1
Printed in China
Book design by: TypeGdesign.com

To order additional copies of this book, contact:
www.pecoff.com
orders@pecoff.com
1-619-964-1990

For everyone

Take a journey with me
in one of these boats
We'll row cross the globe,
we'll sail coast to coast

We'll hit all the spots
where people find spaces
To live in their homes
in unusual places

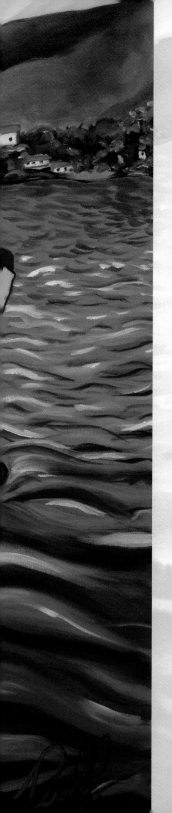

Some people live
on a boat in the sea
Where the air smells of salt
and the winds blow free

When their tummies are hungry
and crave rainbow trout
They cast their line in
and pull dinner out

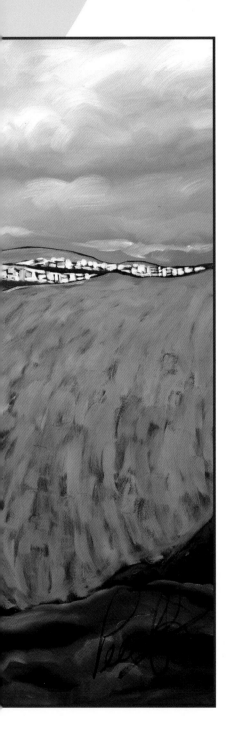

Some people live
near a wide waterway
There's a bridge
they cross over every day

To borrow some sugar
from their neighbor next door
They may have to head
to the opposite shore

Some people live
in a city that's tight
With buildings of every
size, shape and height

They're crammed in together
like teeth of a clown
If one toppled over,
they'd all fall down

Some people live
at the back of their store
Their evening commute
is just through that door

Their job every day
is to give free advice
About amber and mint tea
and sweet smelling spice

Some people live at the end of a pier
Where fishes and seagulls
are always so near

When they want to keep watch
for the visiting whales
They step out the front door
and look for their tails

Some people live
down at the beach
The waves and the sand
are just within reach

The ocean and surf
make up their backyard
Complete with sandcastles
and courageous lifeguard

Some people live
in a temple of gold
A home to some Swamis,
the young and the old

In the palm trees above it
live forty-two geese
Seeking nirvana and
true inner peace

Some people live
in a white-washed mill
Their neighborhood
spreads over a hill

When the wind starts to blow,
the arms spin around
It looks like a pinwheel
attached to the ground

Some people live
over a bustling cafe
Where people drink
coffee all night and all day

When it's time to sleep
but too noisy downstairs
They join in the party and
snooze in a chair

Some people live
in a place in their mind
It's not on a map,
nowhere you can find

The leaves are all flames,
the tree trunks are blue
A place you imagine – these
dreams can come true

So where is the place
that you live, tell me that
A house, an igloo,
a one-story flat?

Tonight as you close your
sleep-heavy eyes
Think of all of the folks
under all of our skies

People who live
all over the globe
Who are going to bed
in their special abode

🐂 Index to Paintings

Cool questions:

If you could travel to any place in the world, where would you go? How would that place be similar to or different from where you live now?

If you owned a store like the Spice Shop, what would you sell?

The sky in the Windmills painting is red. How does this make you feel? How would you feel if the sky was a different color?

If you were the chef at Café Conti, what would you put on the menu?

Find out a fun fact about the place where you live. How does this change how you feel about where you live?

Create an imaginary place to live. Bring it to life in words or art.

For more Open Your Heart activities, please visit www.pecoff.com/funstuff

Fun facts:

The Leaning Tower of Pisa really is leaning. That's because it was built on soft sandy soil which could not support its weight. For ten years, from 1990-2000, a committee worked very carefully to adjust some of the soil to prevent the tower from falling over completely. It worked!

Blue Whales are the biggest creatures ever to have lived on earth - even bigger than the biggest dinosaurs. The heaviest whale ever measured was over 375,000 pounds. That's as much as 25 elephants.

Gondolas, the famous boats used for traveling the canals of Venice are really huge - 36 feet long and 1,300 pounds. That means they are as long as 3 cars and weigh as much as a polar bear. Even though they are so long and heavy, they are easily steered by just one person using only one oar.

The Eiffel Tower is currently painted a shade of brownish-gray. On the 1st level of the tower, there are machines where you can vote for what color you want it to be painted next.

When Layne was a little girl in New York City, she dreamed of living in California. While other girls were playing "House", she played "Malibu" complete with beach towels and pretend sun lamp. She grew up and became a lawyer in Atlanta. She represented the rights of children in court. She was very happy, but everyday she heard California calling. One day, it was time to go.

An artist named Grant had just opened a gallery in San Diego which he lit up with his vibrant paintings of life. Layne was magically drawn to his gallery. Once inside, she was dazzled by the colors and the moment her eyes met the eyes of the painter, they fell instantly in love. 2 months later they were married in a barefoot fairy tale wedding in the South of France.

Today, after 5 years, they are still on an endless honeymoon, traveling the globe. Grant plays with colors, Layne plays with words, and together they play with life. They are currently in the Tropics, making art and inspiring people to live their dreams now.

To purchase Grant's artwork, to purchase additional copies of *Open Your Heart* and *Live Your Dream* or just to learn more about the Pecoffs, please visit:
www.pecoff.com